Pr...

"*The Cannibal Owl* tells a story that resonates ... tion we all have to the soil and the soul of the place we are from while exploring the themes of individualism, loss, and regret, set against a rugged yet ferociously beautiful landscape. One part Jack London, one part Larry McMurtry, *The Cannibal Owl* is a profoundly moving work."

—**S. A. Cosby**, *New York Times* **bestselling author of**
All the Sinners Bleed **and** ***Razorblade Tears***

"Here is a story about the simple things we cannot get away from lest we sacrifice our humanity. A story of growing up, of first love, of the ways we become part of the lives of others and the way they become part of ours. Of compassion and selfishness and hatred and revenge. But most of all, this is a story about loss. The losses that come at the hands of others and those that arrive by our own doing. And finally, of time. Time takes all. Gwyn has given us an American story of a kind now rarely seen."

—**Sterling HolyWhiteMountain**

"Gwyn conjures, with unsparing honesty, an ambitious vision of survival and acceptance. On a scale both intimate and epic, *The Cannibal Owl* immerses us in a tragic, intricate, and incisive dance of power and identity that I couldn't put down."

—**Briley Jones, Editor of** *Yemassee*,
Member of the Comanche Tribe

"Aaron Gwyn is that rarest of things: the genuine article. His voice is his own—American, unafraid, spikily poetic—and in *The Cannibal Owl* he writes like a traveler on a lonely road with no turning till we're all back to the Garden."

—**Darin Strauss, winner of the National Book Critics Circle Award**

"The joy and the job of historical fiction is to bridge the gap in time, and to get us under the skins of those we cannot know otherwise. In *The Cannibal Owl*, Gwyn does just this with discipline, empathy, and palpable affection for his characters. Spending time in Levi's world left me wanting more in the best possible way."

—**John Vaillant, author of National Book Award and**
Pulitzer Finalist *Fire Weather*

Praise for Aaron Gwyn

"Gwyn's novel is a powerful depiction of the rough realities of frontier life, of the vicious influence of racism in a place where 'men who didn't dare look at you in daylight might burn you alive come sundown.'"

—*The New York Times*

"Gwyn creates an overwhelmingly visceral and emotionally rich narrative amid Texas's complex path to statehood. . . . This is a masterpiece of western fiction in the tradition of Cormac McCarthy and James Carlos Blake."

—*Publishers Weekly* (**Starred Review**)

"Gwyn knows how to tell a story—he builds suspense wonderfully. . . . His excellent writing and gift for pacing make this an enjoyable historical novel."

—*Kirkus Reviews*

"*All God's Children* is an enthralling historical novel that presents a vision of the American West. Gwyn's prose is both raw and captivating."

—**Brandon Hobson, National Book Award finalist and author of** *The Removed*

"In Gwyn's expert hands, nothing, including good or evil, is ever so simple."

—**Caroline Leavitt,** *The Boston Globe*

———————————◈———————————

ALSO BY AARON GWYN

All God's Children
Wynne's War
The World Beneath
Dog on the Cross

———————————◈———————————

THE CANNIBAL OWL

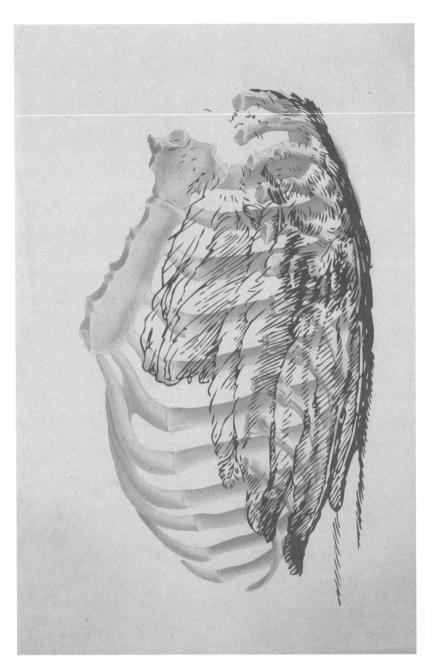

THE
CANNIBAL
OWL

A NOVELLA

AARON GWYN

BELLE
POINT
PRESS

Fort Smith, Arkansas

The Cannibal Owl

Cover image: *Sternum and right side of rib cage.*
Watercolor by G.E. Blenkins after a design engraved by A. Bell, 1831.
(Wellcome Collection)

Edited by Casie Dodd
Design & typography by Belle Point Press

Belle Point Press, LLC
Fort Smith, Arkansas
bellepointpress.com
editor@bellepointpress.com

Find Belle Point Press
on Facebook, Substack,
and Instagram (@bellepointpress)

Printed in the United States of America

29 28 27 26 25   1 2 3 4 5

Library of Congress Control Number: 2024949020

ISBN: 978-1-960215-30-7

TCO / BPP41

—for my goddaughter, Lilah

1

THEY LIVED within earshot of the slap and sigh of that muddy river. Their home was a dugout among the black oak and cedar. Bailey would run his traps before dawn each morning, carrying Levi in a pine-frame papoose. By the time Levi was three he was toddling beside his father through the forests and swirling mists. They trapped beaver. They trapped badger and raccoon, selling the pelts downriver at Le Harpe's trading post, though the Frenchman, by that point, had been gone a hundred years. The post was a two-room cabin separated by a dogtrot. For years, it had been the only settlement in the region. Then, in 1820, Little Rock was surveyed. 1821, the town became the capital of Arkansas Territory and the Pulaski County seat. Levi's father said the country was settling up. Soon there would be more trappers than game.

His mother had died of milk-sick the previous year. To Levi, her passing was like the passing of the moon: she was gleaming; she was gone. The fever that burned through her seemed to make her brighter for a spell. Her face shone like a jewel. Then she was laid out in a cherry-wood box with coins over her eyelids as men filed past, holding their hats.

Later, Levi would wonder if this woman in his memory was the flesh-mother who'd born him into the world, or the story-mother his father talked about—a figure painted on the sailcloth of his skull—and he came to believe Susanna English would return to

1

him someday, just as the moon climbed back into the sky after its absence.

Summer of '25, a week before Levi's eighth birthday, they were coming down the sandstone steps of the trading post when Bailey bumped shoulders with a burly man in a pair of over-the-knee boots. The man's name was Campbell. He was supposed to be a fisherman, though he was known to liberate animals from the snares he stumbled on and keep the pelts for himself—his father's pelts.

"Watch yourself," said Bailey, and when he turned to look at the man, Campbell sank a knife into his belly. Bailey never saw the blade. He thought, at first, that Campbell had struck him with the ridge of his massive hand, then looked down to see a brass hilt flush against his stomach, the bloom of red spreading on his shirt, sticky and warm.

"What did you do?" Bailey said.

Campbell didn't answer, just drew out his knife. There was a sound like cloth tearing, like wet cloth being ripped. Bailey sank to his knees.

Then Campbell was walking down the sward of grass and off into the humid trees. In several minutes, he was gone.

Levi stepped over to his father and saw the man's shirt sagging with blood. His skin was ashen.

"Pa?" said Levi, and then turned to the gallery at the front of the building where a row of men sat smoking their pipes and began begging for help.

His father was dying—did they not see?

The next thing he could remember was a mug of steaming liquid in his hands. Someone was telling him to drink. He sat on a cot in a windowless room that he didn't recall entering. The walls were stained with candlelight. Tobacco smoke hung in the air. He raised the mug to his lips and sipped, something hot and sweet. He looked and saw that his trousers were gone; he didn't know where. He still wore his shirt, but it had copper-colored smears on the sleeves, dry blotches down the front. His mouth tasted like iron. Every so often, there would be flashes of his father, his father's pale face, his placid eyes. He sipped from the mug and the images went away. He stopped sipping and they came back. The liquid scalded his tongue; he sipped until his eyes watered and the roof of his mouth was numb.

Then it was day again, no knowing which, and he was standing beside a pile of red clay as two men lowered the box that contained his father into the ground. His mother's sister had arrived at some point, she and her husband, Joel. Levi's aunt held his hand as the men climbed out of the grave and began to spade the earth. There was a sweet scent on the rotting wind. Flies zagged in and out of his narrow shadow, a silhouette Levi there on the blue ground of evening, his outline in the whistling dusk.

In two weeks, they left for Texas.

2

THE HIDINGS started the day after they reached their headrights near the mouth of the Brazos. Austin's Colony. 177 acres of bottomland, perfect for the cotton his uncle intended to grow. But planting seemed to put Uncle Joel in a brown study, and he'd give Levi a whaling once a day. Twice, sometimes. You never knew why he'd decided to make you bleed.

The man is sad, he beats you.

The man is mad, he beats you.

The man is drunk, he snaps a branch from a willow tree, says, "Strip off that shirt."

Standing there, the switch slicing his flesh, Levi could feel himself drifting. His uncle might be muttering curses, but Levi listened to the speech of clouds, their paragraphs piled on the horizon.

Night nursed him. He was tended by the stars. Come morning, he lay swaddled in sunlight. He felt that his father was living yet. The man had merely dispersed himself. Levi seemed to see him in each silvered leaf, in the light that fell from the hole of the moon. Like Levi's own body, Bailey English had merely receded; Bailey English was everywhere. In the splendor of both sun and moon, in the touch of bare dirt and branches.

In the calls of whippoorwills.

In the cries of owls.

3

S **PRING OF '28**, he ran away. He was only eleven, but life as a prairie orphan beat hell out of fetching food for your uncle's table. There was game here in this wilderness. There was fish and fowl. The deer would walk up to you and stare. Levi ate better those summer months than he had the past several years. Deprived of daily beatings, his limbs began to lengthen. He'd taken his father's musket; he'd taken powder and ball from his uncle's chest. By the end of summer, he'd made his way up the Brazos, past San Felipe, all the way to Groce's Ferry.

There was a log house high on the hill, the largest he'd ever seen. A gallery ran along the front with polished wooden columns. Outbuildings of similar make stood about. Eight of them. Nine.

Below the bluff, cotton fields stretched toward the river. Here, several dozen black men, naked to the waist, stooped with their picksacks while a white overseer in a wide-brimmed hat looked on. This man sat a magnificent chestnut gelding and watched the field hands with a studied indifference, their skin beaded with bright sweat as they pinched the fluff from the cotton bolls and stowed it in the burlap sacks slung over their shoulders.

Levi had never seen slaves before. He didn't understand why folks whose backs were corded with muscle would toil for some slimsy man who lazed on a horse. Then he saw the bullwhip coiled at the overseer's hip, the pistol in his belt.

He squatted there, studying it all with a sick feeling spreading inside him. He wondered what his father would think. He decided he'd ask the man, then realized for the thousandth time he'd never be able to ask his pap another word. He never felt his father's absence more strongly than when he wanted to tell him something.

He watched the men for the better part of an hour, couldn't take his eyes from them. Then he rose and moved on.

A week later, he stumbled onto a band of Comanche out on the broken plains. *Nermernuh*, they called themselves. *The People.* He'd smelled their fire, the scent of sizzling meat, and stalked right past sentries he'd not even known were there—he moved so quietly, the lookouts had neither seen nor heard him—and he was almost in the center of camp before a pack of lanky dogs began to bristle and bark. It was then the braves noticed this blue-eyed boy walking among them, and suddenly they were pressing him on all sides. One snatched the rifle out of his hands before he could even cock the hammer. He was ringed by a cloud of shouting faces, and then he was on the ground, naked in the dirt, his clothes cut from his body as quickly as if they'd been devoured.

Then a man with a deep voice called out and everyone went silent, even the dogs. Levi lay there, staring up at the broad, brown faces. The man with the calm voice stepped into view.

He had a square jaw, a wide forehead, cheekbones high on the cliff of his face. But what struck Levi was his eyes: dark irises with a patina like gunpowder. He reached a hand down and offered it to Levi. Levi took hold of it and was pulled to his feet. The man was dressed like the others—loincloth, buckskin leggings—but the part in his hair was painted bright red, and the braids that hung onto his shoulders were plaited with silver beads. The People watched. It seemed to Levi something important was being decided and the wrong move on his part would result in limitless suffering.

And still, he thought of his rifle. It was a Harper's Ferry Model 1803, a flintlock with the thirty-three-inch barrel, all of his father that remained.

"My gun," he said.

The man just stared.

"Gun," said Levi, bringing his hands up to shoulder an imaginary weapon. "Rifle."

The man's brow furrowed.

Levi made a plosive sound with his lips, imitating the noise of gunfire, and at this the calm man smiled. Levi felt embarrassed, but also that he'd done well. The man turned to speak to the others in a strange tongue, and someone passed him Levi's rifle. He stood there a moment, studying it. Then he presented it to Levi with both hands like a blessing.

Levi stayed in their camp that night, then every night for the next several weeks. When the People struck camp to follow the buffalo, Levi came along. He couldn't understand a word they were saying. He couldn't understand why they fed and sheltered him. He'd let himself wander into their company out of loneliness: he told himself it was the meat he smelled, but it was loneliness sure enough.

He rode beside the calm man at the front of the column. Two Wolf was his name, the band's chieftain, but Levi would not learn this until their words took shape inside him. The People pushed west, men mounted on stallions, women and children on mares. Many of these horses pulled the travois on which the People carried everything they owned: two crossed poles lashed with buffalo sinew and harnessed to the horse, a netting of cloth or leather between the poles, and on this platform stores of dried meat and fruit, buffalo hide and deerskin, stone tools and implements of bone. He saw young children seated on these makeshift sleds, staring back at the land sliding away behind them, the twin tracks of the travois hissing in the earth.

When they reached the banks of the Colorado, tipis were reassembled, doors situated to face the sunrise. Women dug fire pits. Women carried water. Women tried to strike Levi with their whips, but Two Wolf wouldn't allow it. The women complained, saying it was customary to whip captives when they were taken into a band.

He is not a captive, said Two Wolf. *It was he who came to us.*

Levi understood none of this. All he knew was that there was disagreement between these women and the chief. He was housed in a tipi that he shared with Two Wolf's father-in-law, the oldest man in camp. Levi slept beside him on a buffalo skin. His name in the Penateka tongue meant *Group of Men Standing*, but everyone called him Poe-paya. He wore the breechcloth and leggings, but also a shirt of sheepskin that he seldom removed. His silver braids were tied with beaver fur, and in his scalp lock he wore a single yellow feather. He'd been a great warrior in his youth. Now he spent his days making bows.

It was Levi's job to help. This meant fetching Poe-paya his bow staves, fetching Poe-paya his tools. The old man was slow to sit down, slower still getting up. He didn't seem to be in pain, though he walked with a kind of shuffle; Levi had the sense that he'd been injured as a young man and never properly healed.

He walked the riverbanks with Poe-paya at dawn, searching for bow-wood in the stands of bois d'arc and hickory. Poe-paya would stop when he located a likely specimen, then stand there running his fingers along the trunk. If he felt a knot, they moved on. If the bark spiraled, they moved on. You looked for that perfect sapling among thousands of trees, a plumb-straight trunk with perfectly straight grain, free of twist or blemish. When Poe-paya found one, he'd motion Levi up to inspect it. At first Levi thought the man was merely using his young eyes to scrutinize the wood, but then realized Poe-paya was teaching him what to approve of, what to reject.

They'd cut the trees in winter when the sap was down and tote them back to camp. A green sapling was easier to work, but once you hacked it to size, you had to put it up to season. Poe-paya kept bow staves in various stages of completion, hundreds of them. Osage orange. Hickory. Black walnut. Ironwood and ash. Warriors always needed bows: they broke them, traded them; they lost them on raids. And eventually, no matter how perfect the stave or skilled the bowyer, all bows gave out.

Poe-paya would take the seasoned wood, scrape it clean of bark and begin whittling it to shape. Anything you took from the upper limb, you had to take from the lower, right down to the smallest splinter. Poe-paya never hurried. He'd spend hours eyeing a bow stave's belly or sighting along its back. They'd sit in his brush-arbor in the heat of the day, the old man carving with his knife—a few shavings here, a few there—then he'd turn to Levi and pass him the stave, nodding for him to study every cut. When the stave had been shaped to his liking, Poe-paya swiped oil from his nose or forehead and rubbed it into the wood. He rubbed in fat harvested from bear or bison, then put the stave in his tipi to season it further. If Levi had done this work with his uncle, it would have bored him to distraction, but with Poe-paya it was the opposite. Sitting there with the old man, Levi could feel himself returning to his body. He could not have described it, how his spirit left the clouds and branches where it had fled his uncle's beatings and entered his body once again. They spent that autumn making bows, and they spent springtime doing the same. He wore an old buffalo robe that was too large for him, and he was allowed to call Poe-paya *Toko*. His hair grew to his shoulders; Poe-paya wove it into braids.

That summer, there were thunderstorms and lightning. The People were afraid of both—thunder and lightning had no pity—and even Poe-paya's untroubled face turned anxious at the sight of clouds. They did not go to the brush-arbor; they stayed in the tipi, working in the light of the fire. He sat beside Poe-paya, carving a bow stave himself, the man instructing him with a word here or there. *Nahuu*, which meant Knife, and *eetu*, which meant Bow. He knew *kuyunii*, Turkey, and *kwasinabóo*, Snake. *Ekawaapi* was Red Cedar: their tipi poles were made of these. *Aama* was Arm, *Tuhuya*, Horse. *Taibo* meant White Man: when Levi heard that, they were talking about him.

Evenings, other children would come to their tipi and Poe-paya would tell them stories—you could tell they were stories by how his voice rose and fell, the way he'd puff his cheeks or make faces. Levi listened, watching the flames in the fire pit, sparks rising toward the open smoke flaps to the stars. He didn't understand most of what Poe-paya was saying, but he enjoyed hearing the performance in the old man's voice. Poe-paya insisted that Levi sit directly beside him; he was never apart from the man, and even when he relieved himself, Poe-paya was nearby. Two Wolf was chieftain—the band called him

Father—but he was chief only in times of peace; the People looked to another man whenever they went to war. This man was Turns In Sunlight, and though he was always smiling, he was also suspicious, and it had been against Turns In Sunlight's counsel that Two Wolf had taken Levi into camp.

So even during story time, Poe-paya was watchful. Levi was watched by the other children as well. They were never hostile. They were merely curious, as if Levi was an animal they had taken for a pet, even though they weren't supposed to. You kept an eye on such a beast. If something went awry, it would be your responsibility to put him down.

4

THERE WERE SNOWS that winter. Ice hung from the drying racks like shards of glass. He lost track of the days, but by the time there was grass again, something about his standing in the camp had changed, and Poe-paya encouraged him to play with the others. Levi was older than these children, but boys his own age were out trailing birds, shooting bullbats and grasshoppers with their bows, wrestling each other and riding horses. Levi was not permitted to join them. Not yet.

He played with the younger children, boys and girls alike. Poe-paya officiated the games. There were a number of these, but the favorite was *Wasape* or "Bear."

You made a small mound of dirt that was meant to be the sugar. Then the children formed a line facing the mound. Poe-paya drew a ring around the sugar, holding Levi by the heels and dragging him very slowly, his back and shoulders tracing a smooth place in the dirt. This set the children to giggling, and Levi giggled too—first time he'd laughed since his father was killed.

After Poe-paya had drawn the circle, Levi would run and get in line. Soon as he did, Poe-paya became Wasape. The old man lifted his hands above his head, fingers splayed, making a face that caused the children to scream.

His daughter, Morning Star, stood at the front of the line, playing the role of Mother. She was Two Wolf's first wife and Poe-paya's only child, and as Poe-paya reached out and tried to grab them, Morning Star would move to her left or right, trying to protect her children, the boys and girls swinging in behind her. If the Bear caught you, you were eaten: this meant being held to the ground by Poe-paya and tickled until you squealed. The point was to sprint past the Bear and steal a handful of his sugar, and the game went on until all the children were eaten or Wasape's sugar was gone.

Levi loved Wasape. It was his favorite thing that happened. After Poe-paya had used him to draw the circle, Levi would sprint to Morning Star and take cover behind her. She was very lovely, though she had not borne Two Wolf any children; it was because of this Two Wolf had taken a second wife, Slim Grass, who, though older and not as pretty, was already pregnant with the chief's third child. Levi did not know this then. He knew only that Morning Star would protect him from Wasape. Poe-paya grabbed child after child, but never got Levi. Levi and Morning Star had a way of moving together. Levi would dart out from behind her legs, snatch a handful of sugar, then run back and fling it at Morning Star's feet. The woman would laugh and place her hand on his neck.

Such a brave boy, she'd say.

At night, after an evening of this game, Levi would lie awake with his heart beating high in his chest, unable to sleep, unable to think of sleeping. He thought only of Morning Star, how they'd won the sugar. He'd toss and turn on the buffalo mattress until Poe-paya cleared his throat.

Go to sleep, the man said.

Levi couldn't go to sleep. He still felt the heat of Morning Star's palm on the side of his throat. He swallowed very hard, then tossed on the mattress.

Go to sleep, said Poe-paya. *Mupitsi will eat you.*

This *Mupitsi* Poe-paya spoke of was Pia Mupitsi: the Cannibal Owl. The People said this beast stalked the night, searching for bad children. Mother Owl carried a burden basket on her back, and in this basket was a long sharp spike. Disobedient children, children who made trouble for their parents, were taken by Mupitsi, thrown into the basket and impaled.

It made sense to Levi. Mothers said it to their daughters, fathers to their sons.

Cry too loud, Mupitsi will eat you.

Complain too much, Mupitsi will eat you.

Levi's uncle had beaten his hands bloody on Levi's back, but Levi had never seen the People strike their children. Punishment belonged to Mupitsi.

One night, Levi asked Poe-paya if he'd ever seen Mupitsi, prowling the dark.

Poe-paya was silent. His eyes remained closed.

Levi said: *Is the Owl large? It seems if she could fit you in a basket, she'd be larger than an owl.*

Poe-paya said nothing.

Or, said Levi, *do you just call her 'Owl'? And why is she a mother? Is there only one of her, or is she many?*

He was sitting up by this point, staring at Poe-paya.

Poe-paya's eyes opened and he shook his head.

I do not enjoy these questions, the old man told him. *Neither does Mupitsi.*

5

YEARS PASSED them by, summer moon and winter wind, no calendar to mark the months. Dates were heralded by sunlight, strong or weak. He learned the People's language, spoke it even in his dreams. He learned to use the bow; he no longer simply made them. As he grew into his long limbs, he went out with other boys on hunts. They shot birds at first, then antelope and deer. Their camp was on the Pecos now, farther west than he'd ever been. At the age of fourteen or fifteen—he'd lost count of his birthdays—he was allowed to follow Two Wolf on a buffalo hunt, then accompanied him on another several weeks later. That fall, he and the other boys watched the remuda that trailed Turns In Sunlight's war party while the warriors conducted a raid. Levi saw no fighting—was nowhere near the fighting—but the raid was a great success: Turns In Sunlight and his men returned with more than fifty horses that they'd taken from the Tonkawa.

Poe-paya grew more stooped. He was slower to rise, slower in his stride, but every day he made his bows—prized by warriors for their accuracy and strength. Levi still helped him, though he was Levi no longer. He was Goes Softly now. His father had taught him to walk quietly when they checked their traps: you felt the earth with the heel of your forward foot, then rolled the weight onto the ball. By his third year with the Nermernuh, Levi moved in complete and total silence, often startling members of the band, though never, for some reason, Poe-paya. His uncle had beaten him for this—not that the man needed a reason—but stealth was praiseworthy in the eyes of the People, and Levi was pleased to become Goes Softly.

The night after their raid on the Tonkawa, Levi was anything but quiet. He talked and talked.

Poe-paya lay listening to him for a long time. Then he said, *You can tell me more tomorrow. Go to sleep.*

Or Mupitsi will eat me, said Levi, and was instantly sorry.

They lay for several moments in the dark. The fire had almost gone out. Levi's heart beat even faster. Then it began to slow. He thought the old man had fallen asleep. He'd shut his eyes when he heard Poe-paya rising. The man laid a hand on Levi's shoulder and said, *Come with me.*

They went out into summer moonlight, bright as a silver sun. They walked for what seemed hours, neither speaking, the stars wheeling mutely in the sky.

When they reached the escarpment north of camp, they followed it west, the cliff face rising sheer beside them. Levi smelled wet earth on the breeze. He heard the bullfrogs calling from somewhere in the dark.

Then Poe-paya stopped. He stopped, and turned toward the cliff, and stood there, staring. Levi thought he was only resting, but when he followed the old man's gaze, he saw.

Moonlight slanted against the cliff face that rose up to block out the stars. Sandstone, and red clay, and what looked like tree limbs suspended in the striations of earth, but they weren't the limbs of any tree.

They were bones. Levi had never seen anything like them; he'd never seen an animal so large. An enormous skull, ten times as large as any bison's. A rib cage like the iron bars of a dungeon cell; forelegs and rear legs, each the size of Levi's trunk. And in front of the skull, two bones, each curving out like the stave of a massive bow, tapering like teeth or the tusk of a boar. The thrill of fear went through him; the skin on his neck was crawling. He took a step backwards as though these bones might knit themselves together and come to life.

She is not something to be mocked, Poe-paya said. *I have never known a child taken by Mupitsi, but I have seen bones like these since I was young. My own father told me she lives in a cave in the Wichita. The People do not go there.*

Levi stood, blinking in the moonlight. Poe-paya pointed a finger at the creature, tracing her wings, those curved bones stretching out from her skull.

And you can see her basket, he said. *See how it is humped*?

Levi nodded. He hadn't seen wings at first. Hadn't seen a basket. Now the shape formed itself in his mind.

I'm sorry, he said. He didn't know if he was speaking to Poe-paya or Mupitsi. It was not that he hadn't believed his toko: it was that he hadn't seen.

The eastern sky was pink when they returned to camp, and women were lighting cook fires, starting their daily work. Levi nodded off over the bow stave he was shaping, and he nodded off again as they were making glue to apply buffalo sinew to the wood.

Poe-paya shook his head.

He sleeps when he should work, and works his mouth when he should sleep. This is why we warn of Mupitsi.

6

SUMMER of the following year, Levi lanced a buffalo from horseback while moving at a gallop. He was fortunate in the angle and force of the thrust, but that was where his fortune ended. As soon as the spearhead pierced its hide, the buffalo turned sharply and ran its horns into Levi's horse, goring the animal, lifting horse and rider briefly from the ground before all three came crashing down. Levi went tumbling. He saw sky and earth, sky and earth. Then he saw nothing for several moments, and he came to with his ears ringing very loudly. There was dirt in his nostrils and dirt packed in his mouth; he was picking grits of it out of his teeth for weeks. Something was wrong with his bow arm. He couldn't seem to move it.

Then he was being carried. Two Wolf was ordering men about, his calm face looking concerned for once. Levi caught the scent of what smelled like smoke. The sun was hot on his face and his neck hurt. His legs were fine; his right arm was fine. His bow arm was the problem, that and his neck. His ears would not stop ringing. The world moved in flashes and spurts. His blood made its rounds. He would think, *they are carrying me through the grass*, then there would be no grass—there would be bare earth passing underneath him or a canopy of leaves overhead.

At some point he looked up at the man to his left and said, "Put me down, I can walk. It ain't my legs," but he said this in English for some reason, and the man paid him no mind.

23

Then he was in the tipi with Poe-paya. Morning Star was kneeling there beside him. Her face looked very grave, and seeing her expression, Levi became frightened. The buffalo hadn't scared him; the lack of feeling in his bow arm hadn't scared him. Poe-paya watched Levi as he looked up at Morning Star, and Levi's eyes must have betrayed his fear. The old man reached out and placed his hand on Levi's chest.

I have seen much worse, he said. *Two Wolf tells me you brought down a great bull. The men talk of your skill and courage. Tonight, there will be a feast.*

It turned into me, said Levi, but he was thinking that Poe-paya was merely trying to distract him with compliments.

I have seen this happen, Poe-paya said. *I have seen men gored by the animal as they lanced it. I saw a young warrior hurt so badly in this manner that he forgot his death song.* The man moved his hand from Levi's chest to the injured arm: if Levi hadn't been watching Poe-paya, he wouldn't even have known.

I don't know my death song, said Levi.

You will not need it now, Poe-paya said. He got his feet under him and rose to a crouch.

Toko, said Levi, and was ashamed of the note of panic in his voice.

Poe-paya nodded.

Don't leave, Levi said.

I am just putting another log on the fire, Poe-paya said. *Anyway, I would not leave an injured brave to suffer the gossip of women. That is a worse affliction.* The old man smiled, walked to the far side of the tipi, took a mesquite log from a cord of wood, then turned and laid it carefully among the dancing flames. The shadows sawed. Levi realized that it was night.

He dozed off at some point. When he woke, Poe-paya was asleep with his chin drooped onto his chest, but Morning Star was watching over him. Levi studied her for several moments. She had soft eyes and skin the color of parchment. Soft features, hair that looked very soft. But the expression on her face was not one of softness at all; it was one of apprehension. Levi could tell the concern was not entirely for him.

What is it? he said, very quietly so as not to awaken Poe-paya.

Nothing, said Morning Star. She'd been staring off into space. Now she looked at him. *You should rest.*

I am resting, said Levi. *What's wrong?*

The woman's lips tightened. *I shouldn't speak of it.*

Speak of what?

Rest, she said.

They were quiet for a time. Then Morning Star said: *While you and Two Wolf and the others were away, Slim Grass went to Turns In Sunlight's lodge. She went to him for three nights in a row, and then on the fourth night, she went out to her own tipi as her bleeding time had started. I think that Two Wolf knows.*

Levi lay there, thinking about this. Morning Star had called Two Wolf by his name; she hadn't called him *husband*; that was the first thing that occurred to him. The second was that while it was common for brothers to share their wives when one was on a hunt or raid and the other was in camp, Two Wolf and Turns In Sunlight were not brothers.

What will happen?

I'm not certain. I fear it will be bad.

Does Toko know? Levi whispered.

Toko knows one thing only, Poe-paya said, and Levi turned to see the old man staring at him. *Young people talk too much: that is what causes bad things to happen. Young people ought to sleep when it is dark and work when the sun is shining. This is what Toko knows.*

7

BUT THE following evening, Morning Star seemed to have forgotten what Toko knew, and Poe-paya did not interrupt her when she told Levi how Two Wolf had confronted Turns In Sunlight that afternoon in the center of camp, demanding ten horses in damages for his liaisons with Slim Grass. Two Wolf had called Turns In Sunlight *tami*: young brother. It was so common for brothers to share their wives, that a man who bedded your spouse must have thought of himself as a brother—this was Two Wolf's point.

Morning Star said that when Two Wolf called the war chief this, everyone went quiet. Even the wind seemed to take note.

I will not give you ten horses, said Turns In Sunlight. For once his smile was absent.

Then you should not have come to my lodge, Two Wolf said.

I did not, said Turns In Sunlight. *Slim Grass came to visit me.*

You admit your conduct, said Two Wolf, *but refuse to pay its price.* He nodded as if this concluded the matter, then struck Turns In Sunlight a blow upside the head. Morning Star did not see the rock in her husband's hand until that moment. Turns In Sunlight dropped like a heart-shot elk. His eyes rolled back into his head and his legs went stiff, toes pointed in the air as though reaching for something. There was blood coming from a cut on his eyebrow. He lay with his legs twitching.

He's dead? said Levi.

No, Morning Star told him. *He slumbers in his lodge. They say he murmurs against my husband in his sleep.*

Poe-paya grunted.

Levi looked at him. *What is it?*

It is none of our concern, Poe-paya said.

I saw it happen, said Morning Star.

And you were in Turns In Sunlight's lodge to hear his murmurings? Poe-paya asked. *Perhaps you can tell us what he says right now?*

Morning Star blushed, dropping her eyes to the floor. Levi watched her. He watched Poe-paya. He saw the man's expression soften, the tension in his wet dark eyes going gradually slack.

Of course, said Poe-paya, *you are concerned for your husband, and it is natural for women to worry.*

I have seen men worry as well, Levi said, wanting to take the shame out of Morning Star's cheeks.

Only old men, said Poe-paya. *We settle our differences in the Smoke Lodge while boys wait to play pranks on us in the dark. No ones pays us any mind unless we can make them something. But you*, he said, pointing a finger at Morning Star, then at Levi, *the two of you are young.*

8

THE BAND moved back to their camp on the Colorado. By fall of the following year, feeling had returned to Levi's arm, though his neck would ache whenever it was going to rain. He'd get prickling sensations all the way to his elbow, farther on wetter days, down to his forearm or wrist. Sometimes, he'd nock an arrow, draw the bow, and his left arm would begin trembling. He'd put the bow down and sit for several moments, watching his biceps flex and relax, flex and relax. Morning Star said the fact that he could use his arm at all was a testament to her medicine, though Levi said she would have no medicine until her bleeding stopped.

Explain your arm then, she said.

When she spoke to him or he looked at her, his throat would go thick. He'd feel lightheaded and strange, then like he had done something wrong. He tried to focus solely on healing, but these feelings for Morning Star continued to swell inside him. Perhaps she had medicine after all.

Turns In Sunlight was also making a recovery—or his body recovered. But the smiling war chief who was quick to laugh and generous with his game had disappeared; a different person took up residence in his skin. He went around singing, flew into fits of rage and made threats at the slightest provocation. He still rode well; he was still the best shot in camp; but he claimed he could neither smell nor taste, and one day accused a boy of stealing scalps from his shield.

He spent half an hour chasing the youth around camp with a buffalo-scrotum rattle. Then, as suddenly as he'd made his accusations, Turns In Sunlight seemed to forget the matter entirely. He sat down and returned to his song.

It was said he had become a *pukutsi*, one of the crazed warriors who no longer feared life or death. These men were rare, and though the People respected them for their reckless courage, they also knew a pukutsi did everything backwards. To them, the whole world was reversed.

Every day, Morning Star would report Turns In Sunlight's latest deeds to Levi. She told him how Slim Grass had asked Turns In Sunlight to kill a buffalo so that she could make a saddle from its hide. Slim Grass had actually requested this favor long before his injury, but now Turns In Sunlight decided to grant it. He went missing from camp one night. For two weeks, nobody saw him. Then, on the fifteenth day of his absence, Uke was walking past Slim Grass's lodge; he leaned down to the flap and said, *Your pukutsi is back. I think he brought you something.*

Slim Grass hurried outside in her robe, then walked around to her arbor. And it was there, said Morning Star, that she found the skin of a Pawnee man. Not a scalp: the entire skin.

Levi looked at Morning Star. *All of it?*

He even left the hands and feet attached.

Levi tried to picture this.

What did she say?

Slim Grass?

Slim Grass, Levi said. *Did she speak to Turns In Sunlight about it?*

I do not know, said Morning Star, *but she no longer visits his lodge.*

9

WINTER ARRIVED with weeks of freezing rain. Levi and Poe-paya would lie awake listening to the patter of it against the tipi, the sizzle of their fire. When the storms finally passed and the day dawned cloudless, Levi woke to find Poe-paya very still on his buffalo mattress. It was usually the old man who awakened him, and Levi crawled over and sat at Poe-paya's side. The fire was almost dead and a sick feeling tickled his stomach. He placed a hand on Poe-paya's shoulder, expecting to find him rigid and cold, but Poe-paya was neither, and when Levi moved his palm to the old man's forehead, it was hot as a coal.

He fled the tipi and returned with Morning Star. Still, Poe-paya hadn't moved. Morning Star felt her father's face. Her expression became grave and her eyes started to well.

I will get Salted Tail, she said. *Do not tell my husband.*

He'll learn it soon enough, said Levi.

Let him learn it without help from us, she told him. *If father is not well enough to make his bows, the men will turn away from him. His son-in-law will be no different.*

He needs help, said Levi.

Stay with him, said Morning Star. *I'll get Salted Tail.*

When the medicine man arrived, the first thing he did was banish Morning Star from the tipi: Salted Tail seemed convinced that her visit to Poe-paya's home was what had caused his illness in the first place.

Levi watched as Salted Tail folded back the hides of the tipi's floor to reveal soft dirt beneath. Then the man began digging a trench with the stick he'd brought—a shallow ditch a few inches deep, several feet wide, long as a man. When he'd accomplished this, he shoveled in coals from their fire with a spatula of bone, lining the trench with red hot embers, motioning for Levi to build the fire back up while he sang the healing song.

They sat for a time, watching the smoldering grave. The earth dried and began to crack. Then Salted Tail raked all the coals out of the trench and told Levi to put them back in the fire. The ditch smoked and steamed. Salted Tail undid the ties of a deerskin parcel and began taking handfuls of sage from it, lining the trench with the leaves, pausing, at times, to check the temperature with the palm of his hand or to sprinkle water from his gourd to cool it.

He looked up at Levi.

Help me move him, he said.

Levi took Poe-paya's ankles while Salted Tail hooked his hands under the old man's armpits; they lifted Poe-paya and laid him on the bed of smoking sage. Salted Tail tested it once again with his palm, and once more with the back of his hand. Then he rose, located Poe-paya's buffalo robe, and covered the old man to the chin.

He looked at Levi.

Leave us, he said.

Levi spent the rest of the morning in their brush arbor, watching sunlight dance over the river. He didn't see Morning Star. No one came to check on Poe-paya, which either meant she'd been successful in keeping word of his illness from spreading, or she hadn't and no one cared.

Levi worked on a bow stave that was just done curing, but he couldn't get any heart into it, kept thinking about the old man who lay baking inside the tipi. When Salted Tail emerged that afternoon to look for Levi, he found the boy sitting in the arbor, gripping his head in both hands and rocking back and forth.

Salted Tail watched him a moment.

Then he said: *Dry your eyes. This is the last time you will speak with Poe-paya. Is that the face you'd show him?*

Levi followed the medicine man back into the tipi: it no longer seemed like his home or Poe-paya's. It seemed to belong to no one at all.

Poe-paya was lying on his pallet of buffalo pelts. The trench was gone and the skins were back in place on the floor. Levi walked over to kneel beside the old man. He felt himself start to drift. He felt like he was floating. He glanced up at the hole in the tipi, up through the smoke flaps at the sweet fire of the sun.

When he looked at Poe-paya, he saw that the man's eyes were open, those wrinkles deep at their corners. Poe-paya smiled with his eyes now; his mouth was too weak. His voice, when he spoke, was very faint. Levi had to lean close to hear.

Do not look so sad, Poe-paya told him.

I cannot help it, Levi said.

Today, said Poe-paya, *I will walk with my fathers and my body will be young.*

Levi nodded. His throat went thick. Then the smile left Poe-paya's eyes and his expression was urgent.

Hear me, Poe-paya said. *There is much trouble to come. After I am gone, it will not be the same for you here. My son-in-law is brave, but he is a peace chief, and his courage blinds him. He thinks Turns In Sunlight has been made a simpleton. It has not occurred to him that a simpleton may kill you as easily as any other, but Turns In Sunlight is not simple; he has grown spiteful as well. His braves still think him a great war chief, and there are those in camp who say Two Wolf went too far in seeking his damages and is not fit to lead. What they really believe is that if Two Wolf meets an unfortunate end, Turns In Sunlight will reward them.*

If you ask me, I will put an arrow through his heart, Levi said, but his grief had gotten the better of him, and he didn't know if he could actually do this.

Poe-paya's eyes closed and opened, and he gave the slightest shake of his head.

It would do no good, he said, *and worse problems are coming. We have begun to clash with men of your race. Messengers from other bands say we are at war. Some claim we have been at war for years. Your people have not yet discovered how to hunt us, but there are men who are learning. They have studied the Nermernuh's tactics and will use our maneuvers against us. Just as we once did against the Na'isha. This is already happening. I have heard the messengers' stories.*

I haven't heard these lies, Levi said.

They are true, said Poe-paya. *Take my daughter and flee. If Turns In Sunlight rises up, she will be killed along with her husband. If he does not rise, these taibo will kill everyone regardless. Take her and go back to your people.*

They are not my people, said Levi. *I lived with them and they beat me. They make nothing. They killed my father over nothing. They are lazy men who purchase slaves to do their work. You are my people now.*

Poe-paya regarded him out of his dark eyes.

Yes, he said. *I am. But others here are not. Take Morning Star and go. You will be family to one another. I name you as my son and heir. You are strong, and brave; you have no fear of your own death. You have proven this. Make my daughter see that she must go with you. Make this promise to me now.*

Levi sat there. He had many things he wanted to say, but he couldn't seem to create a single word. He had the strange notion that if he lifted the old man and held him very tightly, his toko would not die. He placed both hands on Poe-paya's naked arm, but the old man's flesh was cold as the ground.

Yes, he heard himself say, *I promise,* and then Poe-paya's eyes were smiling once again.

Today, he said, *I will walk with my fathers.*

Levi said, *I would like to walk with mine.*

Yes, Poe-paya said.

Do the taibo go to the Hunting Ground? Does my father live as well? I do not know, said Poe-paya. *I will look for him there.*

10

HE HELPED Morning Star prepare the body. Only Morning Star would assist with the burial; no one else was concerned. Poe-paya had bequeathed all his property to Levi: his herd of horses, his bows and bow staves, his sheepskin shirt. The tipi and his other possessions would burn, and his name would never be spoken by the People again.

They washed the body, painted the face bright red, sealed the eyes shut with clay. They dressed the old man in his buckskin leggings and the moccasins he'd worn every day that Levi knew him, laid the body on a blanket, and then folded the blanket over and secured it with rawhide thongs. When this was done, Levi carried his toko out of the tipi to where the horse was waiting. Morning Star was in the saddle, and Levi lifted the body and got it situated on the gelding in front of her—the old man weighed very little; the fever and Salted Tail's treatment seemed to have burned away his substance. She held her father in place while Levi mounted his pony. He thought the stars looked very bright this evening. Then the two of them nodded to each other, chucked their horses up, and headed north.

There was an escarpment half a dozen miles from camp and they made for it. Here, on the steep slope of the scarp face, were deep crevices made by the weathers. They chose one low on the cliff, a shallow cave that went back into the caliche—you had to stoop to enter. Levi carried the body inside this den, sat it upright against the rear wall so his toko would face the sunrise. Then he sat for several moments until Morning Star called to him.

It was night now. Their forms cast slender shadows across the face of the cliff. It occurred to Levi he must tell Morning Star what her father had said, of the evil coming to camp, how they must make their escape: this would be a fitting testament to the dead. Instead, he worked with the woman in the light of the low moon, constructing a wall of sandstone to seal the old man's tomb. Morning Star carried stones over and stacked them in a pile, but Levi repositioned each of them just so, thought about it and repositioned them again. He would tell her, he decided; he would tell her right now. Then she put down another stone and instead of speaking, Levi took it and found a place for it in his wall. Then another place. Then another. When they were finished, the moon had climbed the sky and their shadows pointed the other direction.

They rode back to camp in silence; Levi would not break it. The trees they passed were like bones; the wind gasping across the prairie was the breath of bones. They could have turned their horses east, and no one would have known; no one would come looking. All Levi needed was to tell her what Toko had said, explain the man's last wishes. But when he tried to formulate the sentence, his mind couldn't find the words; when he opened his mouth, he had no voice. It occurred to him that he loved Morning Star very much. Like a mother, almost. And something else besides.

I will tell her tomorrow, he thought, but it was already tomorrow.

And where exactly could they go? The world of the white man was a world without affection, like living in a land of frozen teeth, whereas here, with the People, he'd had warmth and joy.

They reached camp before dawn, and Morning Star helped Levi carry the old man's possessions out of the tipi: they were Levi's possessions now, though each was a weight to him, each an encumbrance. Then the two of them went back inside for a final time, stacked the rest of the wood on the fire and built it up, brought in branches and brush, filling the tipi until it was alight, an enormous bonfire that brought children out of their lodges to rub their eyes and stare, this early sun, a fuller fire than the one yet to rise.

11

HE LIVED in the brush arbor now. No one spoke to him but Morning Star, though the voice he seemed to hear was Poe-paya's, a whisper in his ears like a constant hiss. He should have told Morning Star of her father's final wish; he should have taken her and fled. He reached down and brushed his fingers over the backs of his legs: the wrinkled ridges of old scars. He could almost feel the sting of his uncle's switch, could almost hear the whirr of it slicing the air. Poe-paya's request had been clear—his response to this request just as clear—but Levi couldn't make his mouth form the words. His lips seemed to belong to someone else. His tongue was an alien organ. He'd begun to retreat from himself, like when his father had passed, but this time it was worse. By day, he watched activities in the camp as though from a great distance. At night, the shadows shrouded him or he lay in a coma of moonlight, sleepless.

Then, not two weeks after Poe-paya's death, the trouble arrived.

There was a light dusting of snow on the ground, and the men of camp sat gathered around a bonfire, smoking cigarettes rolled in the soft leaves of corn shuck. They'd traded with the Comancheros the day before, and all who wanted tobacco had it in plenty. Two Wolf was in an expansive mood, more talkative than Levi had ever seen him. Levi sat in his brush arbor, watching. He watched the chief say something that made the others laugh, but Levi was too far away to hear exactly what. Twilight seemed to dampen the sound. It was overcast and the cover of clouds brought the night on even faster.

Levi noticed Turns In Sunlight just beyond the glow of the fire, approaching Two Wolf from the rear. Too-gah and Always Coughing walked on either side of him. These men carried lances, but Turns In Sunlight held only a long knife. He was maybe ten paces behind Two Wolf when Levi stood and called out.

"*Nahuu!*" he shouted, the first word he'd uttered since Poe-paya's burial. Two Wolf cast him a puzzled look. It seemed as if he'd respond to Levi in his deep, calm voice, but then Turns In Sunlight was standing over him, passing the knife over the peace chief's throat. A streak of blood swept across the skin, dark in the firelight, and then Two Wolf turned and started struggling with his attacker—Turns In Sunlight now slashing, now stabbing, Two Wolf still trying to grapple him.

A musket went off. There were screams. Several of Two Wolf's braves were on the ground bleeding, and then Levi saw half a dozen men charging the bonfire with their lances. He couldn't make out who. He thought, at first, they were coming to Two Wolf's defense, but when the lancers reached the center of camp, they ran the points of their lances through Two Wolf's remaining braves, and then Levi had his bow in one hand, his father's rifle in the other, and he was running out into the dark.

His quiver was on his back—he'd never recall grabbing it and slipping his arm through the strap—and the rifle held a charge and a ball patched in its barrel, but the rest of his shot and powder were back in the brush arbor. The rifle would fire once, and then it would be useless.

He was sucking wind by the time he reached the horses. He'd saddled his gelding and was about to mount up when he thought of Morning Star. Her mare would be with the ponies in the corral on the other side of camp. He stood there, trying to think. She was the wife of the peace chief, and as such would likely be murdered as soon as Turns In Sunlight found her. Provided, of course, that Turns In Sunlight and those who supported him were not killed by men still loyal to Two Wolf. There were shouts and cries in the distance. Levi thought she might be dead already. Then somehow he decided she wasn't. He climbed onto his horse, selected three others—two duns and a yellow roan—and led them out of the corral, steering north toward the rising ground.

When he struck the ridgeline and turned to look back, the sky was black and moonless, and he saw only the glow of the bonfire on that dark prairie. Now and then, the flat pop of musket fire came rolling across the plains. He thought perhaps Two Wolf's men had rallied; he thought Two Wolf's men were dead. Then his thoughts seemed to go out like a snuffed candle, and the quiet rushed in to suffocate him.

He saw that there were now two bonfires burning in the distance. Then he saw there were three. Soon, a dozen fires were blazing, massive lanterns in the night. He breathed for several moments. It took great effort to pull air into his lungs, great effort to push it out again.

He dismounted, and led his horse over to a mesquite and tied it there to a thick limb. He had enough rope to tether two of the others, but the fourth horse would either stand or she wouldn't; there was nothing he could do.

It took him more than an hour to walk back to camp. It might've been longer: he couldn't see the position of the moon. The air was thick and a light rain fell. He sat out beyond the glow of the bonfire, squatting with his rifle and bow. The other fires he'd seen were tipis that had burned: Two Wolf's, Slim Grass's, Walks On Leaves. They'd burned brightly for a while. Now they were just smoldering piles.

Morning Star's tipi stood there untouched. You could see the smoke from her cook fire coming up through the flaps. That she hadn't been harmed was a kind of miracle, Levi thought.

Turns In Sunlight—or a man who, from this distance, looked like Turns In Sunlight—had passed twice in front of Levi's rifle. Levi lined the brass blade of the front sight in the cast steel *V* of the rear sight, and pulled the trigger. The hammer fell; the flint raked the frizzen, but the pan was full of slush, and the weapon wouldn't discharge. He tried again, but it was only a shower of sparks and a wet metallic snap. Turns In Sunlight—or the man who looked like him—disappeared inside his lodge. Levi stood the rifle on its butt there in front of him. He tried, once again, to think.

The gun hadn't fired: perhaps it was a blessing. He could get to Morning Star's tipi without alerting the camp. He thought that if he had heeded Toko's warning, he'd never have known about any of this.

The men in camp had built the bonfire even higher in the time Levi had been gone; it hissed and sizzled in the rain. Two Wolf's body lay there beside it. Levi could see what he thought was Stone Ear's corpse, and then he noticed Hands of Honey and Koe-kay. The rifle was now a ten-pound hindrance; unless he could get powder, that was all it was going to be.

He sat there, wet to the skin, shivering. Now and then, one of the men who'd cast their lot with Turns In Sunlight exited a tipi, walked out to stand beside the bonfire, and relieved himself. One of these men carried what looked like a sack of something and tossed that on the fire. It turned from a sack, in Levi's mind, to a log, but whatever it was didn't catch like timber, and Levi had a sick feeling about it; the feeling traveled low under his skin—beneath the panic, fear, and sorrow—and lodged in Levi's throat. He could smell meat cooking, but it was no meat he'd ever smelled before, and turning his head, he retched.

Morning Star's tipi was perhaps thirty yards away. Turns In Sunlight would confine her to it until he decided to butcher her as well. Levi wanted a knife worse than he'd ever wanted food or water. He could've made do with a club or an axe. What he had was a useless rifle, a half dozen hunting arrows, this bow his toko made him. He wasn't afraid of throwing his life away; he wasn't at all afraid of dying: what he feared was doing it before he could put a ball or blade through Turns In Sunlight's heart. Not murdering his enemy was what terrified him, like an actual hand around his throat. It had less to do with his loyalty to Two Wolf, and everything to do with Poe-paya. He was not supposed to even *think* of the man as "Poe-paya" or "Group of Men Standing"—merely contemplating the name was forbidden.

But Levi did think it—*Poe-paya*—and he decided this was all right. After all, Levi was not one of the People; Poe-paya had told him as much. This realization made him sick all over again, but this time he refused to air his paunch. He swallowed and eyed Morning Star's lodge.

"Poe-paya," he said softly, speculatively, like walking out on the ice last winter when there'd been that cold snap and the creeks had frozen.

Then he was standing. He slung the rifle on his back, gripped his bow and nocked an arrow. There was no one at the bonfire now, and

Levi came forward slowly, moving in a crouch, keeping to the shadows as best he could. The bonfire crackled. It threw Levi's shadow onto the skin of Morning Star's tipi, a silhouette boy sawing back and forth in the light of the leaping flames, outsized and deformed as some beast flown in off the black prairie, Pia Mupitsi whose bones Poe-paya had shown him: the Cannibal Owl.

He advanced on the tipi and his shadow shrank. He knelt there in the mud beside the door and shook the water from his bow. It occurred to him that one of Turns In Sunlight's men might be inside with Morning Star—or maybe more than one. Levi didn't want to think about what all that could mean.

"Poe-paya," he whispered, and then he was praying. He'd never done so before. Now he threw his entire being behind it.

He asked the Spirit to give him speed. He asked to be cloaked in mist. He prayed for the cunning to put his enemies in the ground, to achieve victory this night, or, barring that, to make a respectable end. He addressed the Great Spirit, Our Sure Enough Father, and as he prayed, he seemed to be calling on some amalgam of Bailey English and a face in the sky, Poe-paya blended in there as well: God, and his father, and Poe-paya, that face built of billowing clouds. He did not know where Mupitsi lived, where exactly the Owl made her home, but he asked that this beast be allowed to enter him. He believed such a thing was possible. He was expecting to live several minutes at most. He'd never asked the Great Spirit for help, and he told Him he never would again.

Blind my enemies, Father God. Make their eyes fail at the sight of me. Give Mupitsi leave to swell my soul.

A great calm came over him. He breathed the madness out. But when he drew another breath there was a firebolt in his blood and he felt his chest expanding. His eyes seemed to bulge from their sockets. He gripped the bow, moved the flap of the tipi, ducked, and stepped inside.

The fire in the pit was low. It cast little light, but Levi could make out the bloody lance on the floor. And over on the buffalo mattress, Too-gah lay sleeping. He'd supported Turns In Sunlight during the slaughter, and Levi knew he'd disposed of Morning Star, knew it like he knew this strange breath burning inside him, this fire now in his veins. Too-gah appeared to be drunk, though Levi didn't know where he'd gotten his hands on liquor; perhaps whiskey had been exchanged in the trade with the Comancheros, and Turns In Sunlight's braves had merely saved it for their coup.

The man raised up on one elbow and looked at Levi, but seemed not to see him.

Who is it? he asked.

"Mother Owl," said Levi, drawing his bow. He was staring at the center of the man's chest, but when he released, his bow arm flexed and the arrow struck Too-gah in the throat. The man fell back on his mattress as if he'd been shoved, grasping the arrow shaft with both hands, legs pedaling the air. Levi nocked another arrow, but he didn't fire. He came up slowly and studied the dying man. He set the bow down very carefully, then stepped onto the mattress, straddled Too-gah and sat on his chest.

Too-gah gripped the arrow; he wouldn't let it go. The man was coughing, strangling on his blood. His body struggled with Levi, but his eyes begged for help.

Levi placed his palm over Too-gah's mouth, caught the man's

nostrils in the web of his forefinger and thumb and pressed down very hard.

You are miserable, Levi said. *You will never walk with your fathers. You will choke to death like a woman; I have trapped you inside your bones.*

Too-gah tried to fight him, but he was too weak, and still his blood continued to flow. Levi looked over and saw a long blade lying over on the floor beside Too-gah's shield—a good knife made in a white man's forge, grips of deer antler and a hilt of brass.

Hear me, said Levi, and allowed his speech to darken: *Your spirit will remain inside your body. I will not release it from your mouth. Your name is Too-gah, but you lifted your hand against my People. When you die, I will tear away your scalp, so do not think you enter another life. I am the Cannibal Mupitsi. I will eat your soul.*

12

WHEN IT was finished, he pulled the wet scalp through his belt, slid Too-gah's knife in the belt on his opposite hip. He reached down to pick up his bow and suddenly a great weariness yawned inside him. He could feel it like a cavity in his chest, his shoulders slumping to meet it. Just like that, Mupitsi had departed. Just like Morning Star, Mupitsi was gone.

Levi stood there, trying to get his wind. He was panting. His breath fogged in the air. He'd thought Mupitsi would swell his breast forever; he'd have that lightning inside his bones. Now the ground seemed to pull at him. He retrieved his bow and took a few steps forward, like wading in a current. He'd not be able to kill Turns In Sunlight like this, face down the war chief's band. Either Mupitsi would have to reenter him, or he'd have to enlist the help of others. The only people he knew would now be trying to murder him.

Then he was stumbling across the floor of the tipi. He stooped, and stumbled out into the rain. It was no longer a drizzle. Now it came in sheets. The bonfire was all smoke and hissing steam. Levi went past the row of tipis, then lumbered out into the dark of the prairie, slogging across the fields like a drunk.

By dawn, he was riding again, leading two horses; the one he hadn't tethered was gone. He was cold and very sick, and by nightfall he had shaded up among the rocks with a fever, eating dried buffalo and mesquite meal. He used up the last of this food in several days, and he was unlucky when it came to game. He managed to snare a few squirrels, and he shot a rabbit which he roasted and ate almost whole: meat, bones, and brain.

In a few weeks, he was starving and short of water as well. He led the yellow roan off a short distance from the other horses and slit its throat. He drank all the blood he could hold, collected more in a sack he made from the horse's stomach. He cooked steaks of horseflesh on a spit, jerked the rest of the meat and hung it to dry. He had enough food, but still couldn't seem to get warm. He lay at night with his teeth chattering.

He'd come upon settlements over the next few months, some Tejano, some white. Some admitted him—others turned him away. Men from one camp took shots at him from the gun ports in their walls. He continued drifting. He was convinced Turns In Sunlight was tracking him, and he prayed constantly for Mupitsi to enter him again that he might take his vengeance.

Mupitsi would not enter him.

Mupitsi was a dream.

In every backwater village, every crossroads colony, he asked after the men who Poe-paya had told him about, those companies of whites who rode out to confront the Nermernuh.

February, he was walking the mud streets of Mina in his buckskin leggings and his buffalo robe, still wearing Poe-paya's sheepskin shirt. He'd been told there was such a company here.

Before the Coahuila legislature renamed it in honor of Francisco Xavier Mina, the town was called Bastrop, and it would be called Bastrop again. Levi had forgotten the Anglo preoccupation with names and naming: they called themselves *Texians* now. With the

Nerm, you acquired your name because of something you'd done, and you might change your name by doing something else. But the Anglos and the Spanish pulled their names from a book and stuck you with one for life. On the plains he was Goes Softly, which told you something, while *Levi* told you nothing at all.

He went past the square in the center of town—it had been platted after the Mexican fashion, plotted out on a grid—then along a wide thoroughfare, and there, at the stables, he found the men he sought. He hadn't known what to expect, but it certainly wasn't this: a dozen drunks lazing in stalls like animals, bearded and reeking, no order to their uniforms, no uniforms at all. They smoked cigarillos and grunted to each other, and if they noticed Levi standing there, they certainly didn't show it.

Finally, Levi approached what looked like the largest man of the bunch and kicked his boot. The grunting stopped. The large man was lying against the rear wall of the stable on a mattress of straw with his hat brim pulled down to his eyes. He looked up at Levi and regarded him a moment.

"All right," he said, "what are you?"

"You fight Indians?" Levi said.

One of the men laughed. Several more began to chuckle.

"Why," said the man, "you have depredations to report?"

"I don't know what that means," Levi told him. "I've rode a long ways. I left out, I had three horses. I ate one and traded another for cornmeal. Horse I got left, he ain't going to get me much further. Not in his shape, he's not."

It was quiet.

Then a man said: "You ate your horse?"

"It was him or me," said Levi. "If you all fight Indians, I got some that need it."

A copper-haired man sitting next to the large one said: "Son, we don't just go chasing ever savage God put on the prairie. And don't none of us do it for free. You may enjoy horsemeat, but it's some of us prefer bread and butter."

Levi nodded to a bottle of whiskey sitting there in the straw.

"That's what you enjoy," he said.

"Get your ass out of here," the red-haired man told him, starting to rise, but the large man placed a hand on his shoulder.

"Where's this horse of yours?" he said.

"Waiting outside town," said Levi. "What of it?"

"How old are you?" the large man asked.

"I don't know," Levi said. "I run off years ago. This point, I've kindly lost track."

"Off to where?" said the large man. "Where did you go?"

Levi turned and looked over his shoulder, back toward the daylight, but what he was looking for wasn't lit by any sun. He pulled back his robe, tugged Too-gah's scalp from his belt and pitched it onto the floor. The men stared at it. It looked like a beaver pelt stepped on by a horse.

He said: "I peeled that off a Indian would've put a hole in any three of you. There's plenty more like it, but I can't get them by myself. There's two hundred horses, some of the men got silver. If that don't interest you, tell me where there's somebody it will."

13

THEY PROCEEDED up the Colorado, following it northwest, thirteen riders including Levi, a remuda of horses, their pack animals and mules. The scalp had made an impression. So had Levi's horse when he brought it to the stables: the men studied the faded handprints of dried blood on its hip and stifle, almost black against its chestnut coat. By the time the company passed the escarpment, even the large man deferred to Levi.

The man's name was William Shirley. He was originally from Kentucky, but everyone called him Cajun Bill. He'd lost his wife to yellow fever in the city of New Orleans, 1829. Before that, he'd served in the U.S. Cavalry, Johnson's Volunteers; he'd been there on the Thames River, east of Detroit, fighting the confederation of British and Indians the day that Tecumseh fell. He didn't say how he'd fallen in with a ranging company, or how he'd ended up in Texas. He said no more about his wife. Mostly, he talked about starting a business to transport goods from the Port of New Orleans to San Antonio, but that, he told Levi, would require independence from Mexico. Until then, most of what the Anglos would import from the Crescent City would be supplies to aid in the coming revolution: food, and rifles, and volunteers.

"You have an opinion about free Texas?" Bill asked.

Levi shook his head.

"Sam Houston?"

Levi said he'd never heard of him.

Bill paused and watched Levi a moment, riding there beside him on his Indian pony.

"You don't say a whole lot, do you?"

Levi turned and looked at the man.

"Lord," said Bill. "You got some cold eyes on you, you know that? It isn't an ambush you're leading us into up here, is it?"

"We're the ambush," Levi said.

It took them two weeks to reach that stretch of land beside the river where the Nerm had made their camp, but there wasn't a single soul to greet them that morning they rode up. Just remnants, refuse, the bones of buffalo and the circular patches of scorched earth where the tipis had burned.

The red-haired man spat. His name was Thomas Odom.

"Looks like your Indians have skedaddled," he said.

"They'll be further upriver," said Levi. "This is a winter camp."

"How much further?"

"Another day's ride," said Levi. "We'll do better if we try and take them before dawn."

"Bill," said Odom, "I believe our guide's full of shit." He looked at the man next to him with a bemused expression. He shook his head. "Fighting in the dark."

Bill said nothing. He climbed down from his horse and toed the burnt husk of a tipi. The name of the man it had belonged to was Toward The Moon, but Levi didn't say it.

Bill looked at Levi. "You lived here?"

Levi nodded.

"Until when?"

Levi thought about that. "I'd say three months. About three."

"About three months," Bill said. "And you know where they've moved to. The exact spot."

"I know it," said Levi. "I lived there with them too," and come the next morning when the sky in the east was the color of slate, the men lay on their bellies atop a ridge overlooking the Nerm's camp. They watched the tipis for a while, and then crept back down the hill to their horses, kneeling in a circle while Bill gave them instructions. When he'd finished, the men started to rise.

Levi looked up at their leader.

"It won't work," he said.

"I want you to listen to him," said Odom. He pointed at Cajun Bill. "You have any idea who this man is, you little shit? He was fighting Indians when you were in your pappy's balls."

Bill raised a hand to silence him.

"Why won't it work?" he said.

"Need to stampede their horses," said Levi. "They get mounted, they'll kill us ever one."

"You see this rifle?" said Odom, lifting his weapon.

Levi nodded that he did.

"This'll blow a hole in your savage at three hunnerd yards."

"And then it'll take you a minute to reload it," Levi said.

A man named Hall snorted. "If you're quick."

Odom snapped Hall a look.

Levi said: "These men can put twenty arrows in you while you're stuffing that ramrod down your barrel, and they can do it on horse-back at a gallop."

"Bullshit," said Odom.

Cajun Bill said, "He's right." He stood there brushing his palm back and forth over his stubble. "What's your proposal?"

Levi said he'd go down and stampede the remuda. He said for Bill to pick out his three best marksmen and put them on the ridge.

"When they hear all hell breaking loose with their horses, they'll come swarming out of their lodges yonder. Have your sharpshooters lay into them, rest of you be saddled up to charge."

"Charge," said Odom, shaking his head. "You're about an idjit."

Bill's mouth tightened. "We can't shoot these long rifles from the saddle."

"Won't have to," Levi said. "Without horses, they'll take off running. You can ride right over them. You'll be close enough to use your knives."

"Let me get this straight," said Odom. "You want us to make some kind of half-ass cavalry charge? Have you always been crazy?"

Bill said: "Ronald, Stephen—take your rifles and post up on that ridge. You too, Marlin."

"You're serious," said Odom, and now his voice had fear in it.

"I am," Bill said. "And Tom: if you ain't riding right beside me, you best be running the other way."

14

THERE WERE more horses than he'd expected—a hundred, it seemed—and when Levi lobbed the firebrand into the corral it was like dropping a lit match onto a pile of kindlers. A dozen horses broke through the sapling corral headed north, two dozen burst from the south end of the pen—the animals roiling like flood waters, flowing over each other, screaming.

Levi pulled an arrow from his quiver and nocked it. He moved over and squatted behind a cedar and watched the chaos in the pen, the writhing horseflesh, but all he was really thinking was that riding with the ranging company had diminished him, and that when it came time for Mupitsi to rise up inside his breast, there would be no Mupitsi: just his own fretful heart.

In the corral, horses trampled each other; horses thundered out onto the fields beside the smoking river. He thought of Poe-paya. He thought of Morning Star. He wanted to be filled with Mother Owl's vengeance, and then he breathed the dawn air, cool against his cheeks.

He was two hundred yards from the Nerm's encampment and when he rose and started for it, men were emerging from their tipis. From this distance their figures looked very small; he could cover the entire camp with his outstretched thumb. A few of the braves made for the corral, but the corral, by this point, was nearly empty. Levi watched a man standing in the center of camp. He had the butt of his lance propped on the ground, and had adopted a wide stance, preparing himself for battle. Then he'd pitched forward and was sprawled on his face in the dirt, the report of the rifle that killed him reaching Levi a few seconds later.

If they'd doubted it before, the Nerm now knew they were under attack, and they began grouping up. Levi went trotting toward them. The sharpshooters on the ridge took several more of the braves—the Nerm seemed not to understand where the shots were coming from—and then Levi saw Cajun Bill and his men riding toward the camp at a gallop. They came in from the north, formed into a loose wedge. The sight of the rough men on their charging horse was lovely and terrible, and suddenly the fire of Mupitsi was alive again like acid in his blood. The Nerm let out cries, some loosed arrows, but there was no order to their defense and panic was in the air thick as smoke. Some of the men dashed back inside their tipis: for arms, or their families, or perhaps just to hide.

The two braves who'd started for the corral had turned to watch these mounted white men riding on their camp. Neither had seen Levi, and neither saw him draw the bow and hold it; neither saw him release the string with a smooth slip of his fingers. The arrow struck the taller brave between his shoulders, burying itself to the fletching. The man stumbled, went to a knee, and when his companion turned around, Levi shot him in the stomach. This brave stood there, looking very confused, and Levi nocked a third arrow, released it, but he popped his fingers when he did so, and the arrow hit the man in the shoulder and spun him around.

Then Levi was standing over them. He didn't know who they were. He didn't know if they were new to Turns In Sunlight's band, or if Mupitsi had so changed him, he no longer recognized the men. He could feel the Owl quite strongly, a broad thing squatting on his shoulders, slowly spreading its wings. Levi put another arrow in each of the dying braves. They lay bleeding, but they weren't dead. One moaned softly, the other just wheezed.

Levi mounted the moaner's back and drew Too-gah's knife.

15

HE WALKED into camp to find the battle was over, such battle as there'd been. There were bodies everywhere, few that he recognized. Three tipis were on fire. Odom walked from lodge to lodge with a burning branch. The man would go inside each dwelling, rifle through it, then put his torch to the buffalo hide.

Levi could already feel Mupitsi leaving him, bleeding out as if through a wound. He wanted to find Turns In Sunlight before the Owl left completely.

He located the war chief some minutes later, slumped against a drying rack with nothing but an arrow straightener in hand, the top of his head missing from the brow up, his dead eyes straining as if he was trying to see the injury that had killed him. Levi came up and squatted in front of him. Mupitsi took flight, saw the corpse of her enemy, and sprang into the straggling sun.

There were a half dozen lodges still untouched by fire. Levi could hear the voice of a brave singing his death song. He walked into the nearest tipi and emerged with a quiver of good arrows: hunting tips, very straight, fletched with turkey feathers. He went into the next lodge, and exited with a rawhide sack of pemmican.

The third tipi he entered had been festooned with bullet holes, and lying there on the floor was Morning Star. There was a wound from a rifle ball in the center of her chest, and blood had soaked her deerskin dress so that it looked like a robe of red satin. The air smelled of copper. Levi went to her—hands on her arms, hands on her face, hands everywhere, feeling for her life. Her skin was still warm, but her eyes had clouded, and kneeling there beside her, Levi became dizzy. Then he turned and vomited. Harsh and violent, very painful—like throwing up his soul. He felt something whip through him like a lash, and then he was completely outside himself, watching his filthy body from above, like a bird hovering, looking down.

He was no longer in the tipi. The sky had gone strange. He heard his mouth make a cackling sort of sound. He saw Odom lying on the grass, staring up at him. He realized that he'd put the man there, but he didn't recall how. Odom's torch was in Levi's hand, and he was squatting on Odom's chest, trying to shove the end of the flaming branch down the man's throat. Odom was screaming, clawing at Levi's face, and then there were hands restraining Levi, pulling him back.

Bill had him in some kind of hold. The man was saying, "It's all right, lad. It's all right," whispering this in his ear, over and over. Levi bucked and struggled, but Cajun Bill was very strong.

I wanted to find my people, he heard himself say, then realized he'd spoken in Comanche and they'd just killed everyone who might have understood him.

And then he saw it: his entire life spooling out in front of him on the horse-trampled earth, an existence with these miserable, muddy men, no better than beasts. He closed his eyes and his body began to shiver. He could see his mother's face very clearly, though it seemed she'd been dead a thousand years, and then the face of his father, the faces of his uncle and aunt. He knew he would live for a very long time and he thought the Great Spirit had granted him this as an affliction.

"I wanted to find my people," he said, and Cajun Bill tightened his grip.

"Hush now," the man told him. "Shhhhh."

16

THEN HE was old, seventy-seven, seventy-eight, older than his *toko*, twice as old as his father ever got to be. The year was 1894. He couldn't recall a thing he'd done.

He lay on a bed in a dim room, his body like a bundle of sticks, almost nothing to it. He had the forgetting disease. People would come into the room, sit in the rocking chair beside the bed, and tell him about his life.

"You were commissioner of Atascosa County," they'd say.

Or, "You were captain of a company of Rangers."

An old man walked into the room one morning and handed him a badge made out of a Mexican coin.

"That was yours," he said.

Folks would tell him how he'd helped settle Dimmit County or how he'd founded the town of Carrizo Springs, but he recalled none of this.

Nor did he care.

He was only trying to remember the before-times, trying to recall his mother's name. He still believed that she'd return.

He found that it was very hard to get his breath. There wasn't enough air in the room or his lungs were too weak to draw it. Men stepped up to either side of the bed, lifted and propped him against the headboard on pillows.

He looked from one to the other—didn't recognize them, but they had his eyes.

It was night now. Oil lamps threw shadows on the walls. He closed his eyes and opened them. Closed and opened. The room seemed to grow darker and a passel of folks had crowded into it, waiting for something, their faces frozen in expectation, but none of that concerned him anymore.

What was her name?

The ceiling was yellow in the lamplight. He studied it as he struggled to draw his breath. He closed his eyes and when he opened them, the ceiling was no longer the ceiling, but branches and stars.

He lay there, watching. His breath came easier.

He was in the room and he wasn't. He was in a bed and he wasn't. His spirit had begun to swell, filling the corners of night. The branches canopied the darkling sky.

And there, very high, a shape was circling, blacking out the stars as it passed beneath them, growing larger as it drifted down. Levi felt like a child again, a small child in a pine-frame papoose, riding on his father's back as the man moved through the mists beside the rushing river in the predawn dark. Above them, the shape was gliding just over the treetops. He could make out her face and then her name blossomed suddenly in his mind. He raised his hands to greet her, and she swooped down to gather him, opening her talons, extending her wings.

Acknowledgments

I would like to thank my editor, Casie Dodd, and the staff at Belle Point for their attention to this work. Thanks also to Peter Straus, my agent for ten years. My good friends Ben Avery and Ashleen Menchaca-Bagnulo were kind enough to critique the manuscript, and I was greatly honored to have Comanche Tribe member Briley Jones read *The Cannibal Owl* and offer notes on the language and customs of his people.

AARON GWYN is the author of a story collection, *Dog on the Cross* (Algonquin Books, 2004, finalist for the 2005 New York Public Library Young Lions Fiction Award), and three novels: *The World Beneath* (W.W. Norton, 2009), *Wynne's War* (Mariner Books, 2014), and *All God's Children* (Europa Editions, 2020, Winner of the 2021 Oklahoma Book Award, longlisted for the 2022 International Dublin Literary Award, and finalist for the 2021 Reading the West Award). His short stories have appeared in *Esquire*, *McSweeney's*, *The Missouri Review*, *Glimmer Train*, *Virginia Quarterly Review*, *Gettysburg Review*, and the anthologies *New Stories from the South* and *Best of the West*. His narrative nonfiction, journalism, and articles have appeared in *Esquire*, *The Huffington Post*, *The Missouri Review*, *Swamp Pink*, *The Spectator* and anthologies from *Creative Nonfiction*. He lives in Charlotte, North Carolina, and is an associate professor of English at the University of North Carolina-Charlotte where he teaches fiction writing and contemporary American fiction.

Belle Point Press is a literary small press
along the Arkansas-Oklahoma border.
Our mission is simple: Stick around and read.
Learn more at bellepointpress.com.

BELLE
POINT
PRESS